# THE ARRANGEMENT 20

## The Ferro Family

By:

H.M. Ward

www.SexyAwesomeBooks.com

# COPYRIGHT

H.M. WARD PRESS
First Edition: August 2015
ISBN: 9781630350765

# THE ARRANGEMENT 20

## Dear Reader,

The Arrangement Series is different. How? The story is organic—and growing swiftly. Originally intended to be four serial novels, fans of the series demanded more Sean & Avery, spurring an entirely new concept: a fan-driven series. When fans ask for more, I write more.

I am astonished and humbled by the response this series has received. As the series grows, I am constantly fascinated by the requests and insights from readers. This series has sold over 10 MILLION copies! The average length of each book is 125 pages in paperback and can be read in a few hours or less.

This series intertwines with my other work, but is designed to be read independently, as a quick read between other titles.

You can join in the discussion via my Facebook page: www.facebook.com/AuthorHMWard.

For a complete listing of Ferro books, look here: www.SexyAwesomeBooks.com & click BOOKS.

Thank you and happy reading!

~Holly

## Chapter 1

My muscles twitch, desperately trying to react. I want to run to Sean, but, in my mind, I know he's already dead. The gunshot still rings in my ears. I know there's nothing I can do. Rushing to him will kill us both, and still I struggle to keep my feet planted.

The shore in this spot is away from the houses. There's no one to hear us. No help is coming. The roar of the ocean muffles the sound. My chest feels as if it's being crushed from within. I can barely breathe.

I want those final moments with Sean. Just as I decide to rush to him, consequences be damned, more gunshots ring out. My body stiffens. The noise pierces the night sky, echoing guiltily in my ears. My stomach tries to climb into my throat, and I know the expression on my face gives away my true feelings. I'm frozen in a silent scream that won't end.

The only thing working in my favor is uncertainty and my brother's need to humiliate me.

Vic turns toward me, the wind blowing his shirt open, making him look like a hero rather than the deranged murderer he is. His expression is smug, so arrogantly certain of himself. His hands are casually shoved in his pockets and a triumphant smirk crawls across his lips. I can clearly read his thoughts on his face—he thinks I'm weak. He thinks he's won.

"The Ferro family has fallen," Vic says, projecting his voice across the beach to make sure his men can hear us as well. "By the end of the day, you'll wish you were with them, little sis. Revenge isn't my thing—but seeing you suffer—that I'd like to watch. Care to see the remains of your boyfriend?"

I can't see Sean from here. They dragged him behind a dune where the shoreline curves out of sight. In my mind, I can see the sand stained with blood and Sean's vacant eyes.

Gasping, I fall to my knees in the sand. I'm unable to wipe the horror from my face. Vic thinks it's because his men put a set of bullets in Sean, but it's so much more. Despair is creeping around my throat, threatening to pull me under.

Vic kicks sand at me and laughs.

"You're pathetic."

His words sound like buzzing and hold no meaning. He continues with his harsh tone, but I can't hear him. My guts feel as if they were ripped from my body. I'm fighting an internal battle and losing. My chest screams from the anguish of losing Sean. Death rips me in half, from nose to navel. I can't hold myself upright any longer. I fall forward and gasp, trying to breathe.

The air has turned toxic. It fills my body with a poison I can't expel. My mouth waters as my throat tightens. My stomach twists as it plummets into an unending freefall. I can't control my reaction. It's consuming me. Vomit creeps up my throat and I can't hold it back any longer.

Uncontrollably, I spew my stomach contents onto the sand in front of me. When there is nothing left, I dry-heave until blood vessels pop. My vision blurs and I press my face to the sand.

Vic turns his back to me, leaving me wallowing in misery, and begins to bark orders as he walks down the beach. There are about one hundred feet between me and the dune by the shore. The wind blows the grass plants behind me. They divide the ocean from the marshes on the other side of the beach.

Angry tears roll down my cheeks. There's nothing I can do to stop Vic, nothing I can do to fix this. Sean is gone. He's dead. I'll never see him again.

Every inch of me is coming undone, pulling apart seam by seam. There's nothing left of me—my life is over.

My stomach contracts and forces up air as I wretch again. Sweat covers my skin, clinging to my face as I clutch the sand. The harder I try to grab it, the more it forces the grains between my fingers. In this moment, nothing is real; even existence is beyond my grasp.

I feel everything and nothing. The wind swirls around me, licking my glistening skin, whipping strands of hair into my eyes. They flutter there, suspended in space, frozen in time as I stare at the waves pounding against the shore. The roar of the ocean should be loud, but I don't hear it. The cries of the seagulls sound as if they're far away, trapped in another world.

This can't be happening. After everything we've been through, it can't end like this.

Sean was my other half. I wasn't certain until this moment, but I am now. In a world of horrors, he was my light. It didn't matter that he was shrouded in darkness. For some reason, he still shone brightly around me. I could see the real man—the one beneath the shadows and behind the pain—and now he's gone.

The sky churns like my stomach, swirling clouds into an angry mess. The bottoms of the clouds are ominously dark, evil like my brother.

I sense something in Vic, something that sets my hair on end and makes my skin turn to ice. Sean thinks of himself as a monster, but he's wrong; his actions are born of love. Sean protects his family, even when they don't notice. Vic is on a power trip and thrives on the rush. He won't stop until every Ferro is dead, or worse.

My chest tightens with the realization of that truth.

I watch Vic's back as he recedes and wish to God that I could hurt him. I want to claw off his face and make him scream out in agony. My rage is pent up, unfocused and building. My hands shake as I breathe in and exhale loudly. My nails dig into the sand and squeeze hard.

Body poised to launch at Vic, I push myself up slightly, intending to spring forward.

He'll shoot me before I reach him. His men will stop me. There's no way my hands will ever wrap around his throat, but I have to hurt him. I need to feel my nails rip that arrogant smirk off his face.

Before I can move, something grabs my ankle and pulls me backward. Sand forces its way into my mouth as I'm whipped with dune grass. I'm dragged over the dune and down the other side. A hand clamps over my mouth, stifling my scream. I can't see who it is—they're behind me. I part my lips and bare my teeth. I'm done with this. I'm going to bite their fucking hand off.

A familiar voice whispers quickly, "If you use those K-9 fuckers on me, I'll throw your sorry ass back to that deranged shithead." She whirls me around but keeps her hand in place.

Mel's eyes scan the crest of the dune, her hand still clamped over my mouth. "He has one fine ass, though. Why are all the hot ones insane? Is that like a Darwinist thing? Survival of the sexiest?" Mel looks down at me and sighs. "You're one lucky chick, you know that? I've been following you. If I hadn't, well, you'd be going home with hot pants over there. I heard he's a sick fuck, but damn." She draws out the last word, making it multiple syllables before looking at me once more.

"Choose your poison, Avery—me or him?" She pulls her hand away from my mouth and sits back on her heels, allowing the dune to hide us from sight.

Mel's dressed in a black sweatsuit with the hood pulled up, her hair slicked back beneath the thick fabric. Her trademark hoop earrings are missing, as is the normal bling that's all over her fingernails.

With my heart pounding wildly, I make my choice.

"You."

Mel's golden eyes glance around before she nods.

"Then follow me."

## Chapter 2

My heart is in my throat. I follow Mel blindly, unable to see in the seemingly endless darkness. Even though we're moving parallel to Vic, we're still too close to him to feel at ease.

I want to ask Mel where she's been, but I'm afraid of the answer. Mel is more of a sister to me than I thought possible, but Sean's claims that everyone around me was a plant echo through my head. If Amber was a cop, maybe Mel is, too. It'll suck if she's been lying to me this whole time.

We snake around the spot where everything went wrong. I can see Sean slumped face down in the sand, cold and expressionless.

Oh, God! His death is my fault! I press my eyes closed and try to stop the tears. I need to see right now, and big snotty sobs aren't an option.

Mel elbows me. She presses one finger to her lips, another toward the marsh. I nod, thinking that we're heading toward a boat or something. When Mel walks straight into the slime and reeds, I realize no one is picking us up. The water comes up to my chest as she leads me slowly through a maze of reeds.

My clothes stick to my skin and the cold water chills me until I'm numb. I like the lack of feeling; it's familiar and comforting.

We wade through the muck, slowly, carefully, steering clear of the boat paths cut into the marsh. Nearly to the opposite shore, gunshots crack through the night from behind us. Mel freezes. We wait and listen, hearts pounding.

Mel holds up a hand, signaling for us to be still. Her eyes dart back and forth as she listens.

Birds rustle the reeds reacting to the gunshot. As they settle back in or fly away, the only thing I can hear is the hammering of my heart.

Mel's gaze locks with mine. It's too wide, too panicked. My lips part, ready to speak, but she shakes her head slowly.

Just then a light sweeps over our heads. Mel grabs my shirtfront and pulls me close. We sink down in the water, leaving only our noses above the waterline.

Mel presses her eyes closed and forces her breathing into a slow, steady rhythm. I'm ready to suck up swamp water and scream. The beam of light goes right over our heads again.

That's when we hear voices.

"She couldn't have made it far." The irritated male voice is deep. He's close.

The sound of water splashing fills my head. Someone is wading into the marsh. My insides twist as a scream builds inside of me. I lock my jaw and try to swallow it back.

"Do you think she's out here?" His voice is higher, uncertain if he should wade in further.

The light sweeps over us once more, slower this time. I close my eyes and count. That scream is ready to explode. I mash my mouth together and keep counting.

FOUR

FIVE

SIX

The light sweeps over us, again, moving so slowly that I'm sure he sees us. The beam slices through the darkness, creating shafts of light between the reeds. There's no way I blend in.

SEVEN

EIGHT

The beam slowly drifts to us again and holds.

NINE

TEN

Shit, shit, shit! He sees us. He has to.

Mel's grip on me tightens. She's completely still, barely breathing.

The light clicks off.

"Nah, the only thing left in this shit-hole is the body we put here. Come on." Water sloshes noisily as the man makes his way out and they move on, their voices receding into the distance.

## Chapter 3

"I can't believe your hide-out is the basement of the dorm." I glance around after toweling off my hair. Mel is sitting on the floor, pulling on her sneakers. She yanks one lace tight and peers up at me.

"I think the words you are looking for are THANK YOU. Otherwise, your sorry ass would have been all covered in slime and growing shit."

"Thank you. And gross."

"Maybe," Mel says with a half-laugh, "but nobody goes into those marshes unless they're totally fucked."

"I can see why. I have slime in places I didn't know I had. Plus the bug bites on my chest make me look like I have five tits. It's classy." I stare down at my girls and poke at the itchy lumps next to them.

Mel laughs. "A girl's gotta do what a girl's gotta do."

I nod and smile. I'm trying to act like nothing is wrong, like we're old friends, but my mind has been screaming at me to get away from her. Mel has offered no explanation of where she went or who she works for. I'm beyond hysterical. I'm in that place where everything melts into one big ball of crap. I have to find Peter and Jon before Vic does. I can't waste time hiding out with Mel, waiting for this shitstorm to blow over.

Based on the boxes around me, and the way the room is laid out, she's hidden down here before. I can't blame her. It's got central air, only one entry point, and the showers are only one floor up. I stand up and poke around in the boxes.

"So is all this crap yours?"

She shakes her head and pulls her other leg into her chest. "Nope, this is shit that gets left upstairs. At the end of the year, after everyone leaves, the stuff people forget or abandon gets tossed down here. It's held for the next school year and then sold off in the summer."

"So no one comes down here?" I find a box of stuff that was probably owned by a guy. I lift a grease-covered Chilton's manual when I spy something else in the box that is actually useful. I need to figure out how to get my hand on it without Mel seeing.

"Not really. Only the custodian, Ernie, but I pay him to look the other way. He'll do whatever, as long as he gets his part. Happy times." Mel pulls her laces tighter, X by X, so the tongue of the shoe is no longer visible.

"Do you think you have them tight enough?" I say it deadpan and drop the manual back into the box. I manage to wrap my fingers around the item I want before she looks up.

"Smart ass. I've got narrow feet. I hate wearing these things. They never fit right." She wiggles her foot in the shoe and starts over. "That's better."

"Yeah," I smile and lean on a box next to her. Mel is blocking the only exit. "About all this," I begin, gesturing around the room. "Thanks for saving my ass, but I need to finish something." Just as I move my foot to step past her, Mel jumps up.

"Yeah? Where are you going this time, to beg Black for help? Or are you trying to find the remains of Constance Ferro?" She leans against a tower of heavy boxes and folds her arms over her chest. I've never seen Mel with her hair slicked back. It makes her eyes look like they belong on a tiger. I half expect her to bitchslap me with her paw—uh, hand.

I'm hiding the little can of pepper spray in my palm. She doesn't see it. This is going to suck. I really don't want to Mace her.

"How long have you been following me?"

Mel looks annoyed. She straightens and steps closer. I should spray her now and run, but I want to know what she's going to say.

"Why do you walk straight into shit that's so far over your head, there ain't no way you're walking out alive? Every goddamn time. You're like a suicidal poodle running across the LIE at rush hour. What the fuck, Avery?" She says my name in three syllables and cocks her head to the side.

I stare blankly at her. This girl was my friend, she watched out for me, but she also brought me to Black. I can't ignore that part. She played me.

"Maybe I have a death wish."

She laughs like that might have been funny at one point, but that time has passed.

"Maybe you did, but not now. Not post-Sean Ferro. So what's your plan? If you walk out that door alone you're dead. And then all this was in vain."

"All what, Mel? What exactly have you been doing this whole time? Are you a cop? Have you been trying to nail me for something?" I want to scream, but I keep my emotions in check. Mel's smart. I can't lose it, not around her.

She smiles and leans in close to my face. She looks into my eyes like they're little windows and she can see someone inside them looking out at her.

"Hello?" She yells and then knocks on my forehead. "Where the hell did Avery go? All I see is a dumbass white girl here now. Kinda looks like Avery, but the brain is broken, stupid as shit."

"Don't be an asshole," I say, swatting at her hand. "You know what's going on, and you've been pretending to be a student, struggling like me. The truth is you aren't like me at all, and I won't stay here just to listen to more lies."

Mel's smile widens with amusement at my sudden backbone. When I lift the pepper spray to her line of sight, her grin falters.

"Shit, no! You ain't gonna spray me with tha—"

When she starts speaking, I press down. Hard. The button slips past the safety and the little can starts to hiss, but nothing comes out. I make a growling sound and scream. "Why does this always happen to me?"

Mel is laughing. Before she sees it coming, I wind up and throw a punch straight at her face. The little plastic bottle connects with her temple. The smile flies off her face, leaving her glaring at me.

"Oh, no, you di'n't!" Her head sways as her gaze narrows.

The tiger is going to rip my head off now.

I turn to run, but there's nowhere to go. I crash into a tower of boxes and duck behind them as they topple to the side. Mel evades them and is on my heels, swiping at me, yelling as she chases me in circles. "What the fuck is wrong with you? I've never done a damn thing to you!"

Panting, I yell back, "You sent me to Black! You're full of shit, just like the rest of them!"

I swat at a bike that's leaning against the wall and toss it down. It clatters when it hits the floor. Mel swears and stops to pick it up. I pause behind a six-foot tower of boxes and watch her.

"What do you want me to tell you, Avery? The truth? Or more shit? I hate Black. I always have, but the woman has the right connections. I am a dumbass college kid, just like you. I stepped into a shit-storm when I met you. Since then Black has had me watching you. Then I found out what she really does." Mel goes pale and shakes her head. "That's some messed up shit. You ever wonder why there's a call center in that building? Did you look around?"

"Yeah, it's a front."

"No shit, Sherlock. But a front for something worse. If they find her hookers they think they nailed her, but that's not how she makes her money."

My lips part and I want to ask, but I'm not sure if I want to know.

"Tell me."

"It don't matter," Mel says shaking her head. "As long as we keep playing dumb and acting like we don't know—"

"I don't know!" I step out from behind the box and start talking with my hands. Once I begin, I can't stop. "I don't know anything anymore. My Dad, the one who loved me, wasn't my real father. My brother is freakin' Vic Jr. I had no idea. I see nothing! I know nothing! And I'm sick of it. So, spill! Tell me why you're following me, why you're here now, or walk away."

The corner of her lip lifts and then falls quickly. Mel sighs and nods.

"Fine, have it your way. I started with Black the same way as you—a friend brought me in. We're there together until last summer and then she takes an internship overseas. When school started this year, she didn't come back. Black said she moved on to bigger and better things. I assumed she found a real job. Fast forward to you. I think I'm helping you by bringing you in. Black must have been eyeing you for other reasons, but I don't suspect that then. She gives me a kickback every time you work. So I encourage you to keep at it."

"Gee, thanks."

"Surviving justifies anything. I already told you that, and I'm not apologizing for it." Mel clears her throat and sighs. "The thing is, as I work less, Black shifts my job. Now instead of the random fuck, I'm moving cargo and checking spreadsheets. It's an OCD wet dream."

"So you love it?"

"Yeah. It gets me outta doing the nasty while still earning the same money. It's a good gig. I know it's too good to be true now, but at first I thought the same as you—the call center is a cover for the brothel. Since I'm stepping up, I don't care. Add in the dead hooker and I really don't want to go back. Black makes it seem like I'm looking out for you, the way I would a little sister. Since I feel that way about you anyway, I didn't see it as a bad thing. So, I followed you. I watched you with Marty. I found out way too much shit about Marty." Her face goes blank for a second and then she shakes her head as if trying to dislodge a thought. "That boy has issues."

"I know. Back to Black, please."

Mel looks at me from under her brow. "You know he's not a fairy, never was?" I nod. "You know he was working for Victor? And that he was supposed to slit your throat when you got hot and heavy?"

"Yes, get on with it." Mel makes a face and waits. "What?"

"You forgave him? What the hell? You seriously let that little fucker off the hook? He's been following you around so he can kill you. He was a fucking assassin hired by a mob family, and you're still acting like he's a harmless puppy!"

"No, I'm not. I know what he is, what he's done, and what he does. What I don't know is anything about you."

"Me?" She presses her hand to her chest. "Me? You think you don't know me? What about you, Avery? I thought we were friends? Then I find out from someone else about all this shit. You didn't tell me anything! You slept with Trystan Scott! You never even said anything. He's a fucking rock star and you nailed him and said NOTHING." Her jaw locks as she stares me down.

I can't help it. I smile. "That topic is a little intimate for a total liar."

Mel sucks in air through her nostrils, flaring them as she breathes. "You did not go there. I swear to God, Avery—"

"Stop swearing and just do it! If you're here to drag me back to Black, do it! If you're here to shove a knife in my heart, stab away! I can't take this anymore, and I sure as hell can't beat the knife ninja to even get past the door." I step out from behind the boxes and face her.

Mel watches me closely, her eyes flick from my hands to my feet and back to my face. She anticipates an attack. Her body says as much. I sit down on the floor and hold my hands up.

"I'm done," I say wearily. "I'm not fighting you."

Mel hesitates. A moment later, she says, "I'm not here for Black."

"Then who are you here for?"

A deep voice comes from the hallway. "Mel works for me."

## Chapter 4

Gabe steps into the room and spots me on the floor. I'm sitting cross-legged and leaning back on my hands. My confusion leaks onto my face.

"I'm sorry, what?"

Gabe smiles at me and shakes his head. "You don't listen for shit, you know that, right?"

I can't help it. I smile. "My dad used to say that."

Gabe walks in, dressed in his usual sleek suit. It's a little big for him. He opens his lapel and pulls out a wallet. A moment later, he's handing it to me.

"You're on the cusp of something so much darker than a Ferro could ever do to you. Open it."

I feel the cold leather in my hands, and flip it open. A gold badge shines under the bare bulb. I glance up at him again.

"You're a cop?"

"FBI."

"That's the wrong jurisdiction for prostitution, isn't it?" My eyes bounce from Gabe to Mel and back to Gabe. "You guys don't do that. Why are you watching Miss Black?"

Gabe pulls a folding chair down from the stack of crap along the wall and opens it. He sits down and takes off his jacket, placing it neatly on his lap.

"When I started this case, I thought I knew what I was walking into, but I had no idea. It's so much more than we originally thought, and Black is careful. That woman covers her tracks. We haven't been able to nail her on anything but prostitution. When first looking at her business, it's designed to reveal an active madam who sells girls for five to six figures. She has specialty clients—high profile. It's the kind of establishment that a DA would take down with pride and never assume there's something more nefarious going on. But there is. People started disappearing over the past few years. Multiple women."

"Where'd they go?" I ask, looking over at Mel, who is uncharacteristically silent.

"It's not a pretty story, Avery. It's the kind of thing that gives me nightmares, and I've seen more than most. But this? What Black does? It keeps me awake at night." Gabe pauses and shudders as if overcome by a disturbing memory.

"I was lucky she wanted you." Mel swallows hard. "You know how she was suddenly very interested in your virginal situation, right? Well, it turns out that fetishes are her specialty. If you've got enough money, she'll make it happen. That side of her business soon outgrew the regular side. And when a girl comes in and gives free reign the way you did, she knows you'll go all the way."

My stomach dips and I resist the urge to squirm.

"What are you talking about? I did go all the way. Sean is—"

"Sean Ferro is not her target clientele. Not anymore." Gabe exchanges a look with Mel.

"Tell her. Otherwise, she'll walk into it and not know what's happening until it's too late."

"I'm not selling myself again," I say with a laugh. This is absurd. "After everything that's happened, you really think that I'd—"

"I really think you'd end up asking Black for help. Yeah, I can see that. With Constance Ferro dead, and Sean… I'm sorry, but you're in a bad place. I can see you asking Black to help you crush Vic and I can see her saying yes because she wants you." Mel says it carefully so I don't lash out.

"Wants me for what? You keep saying Black's hiding something. Who cares about fetish clients?" I glance at Gabe.

He takes a deep breath and leans forward putting his elbows on his knees. He's close enough that I can smell him now, aftershave and Tide. His badass vibe mixed with his squeaky clean smell suddenly seems funny.

"That seemed to be the start of it," Gabe begins. "Black entices guys like Sean Ferro with beautiful women, then appeals to their darker sides—their need for something beyond what is acceptable."

Fear rushes through me as ice climbs up my spine. He knows. He knows what Sean did to me, what he did to the others. The monster isn't a secret. I try not to show my feelings on the subject.

"And…"

"And Sean Ferro is a pussy cat compared to what else is out there. Black finds girls who give no limits and offers them positions of power while ensnaring them with contracts and payment advances. It seems like something minor at first—maybe succumbing to fear—but then she passes them through a chain of clients, in order from most timid to most extreme. Women were abused, raped, scarred, starved and beaten within an inch of life. Some guys went too far. Black knew they would and did nothing to stop it."

Horrified, I sit there and stare at him. "That can't be true. She said she does background checks. I saw them! Then there's you, the other thug, and the bracelets. When I was in trouble, you were there."

"It's all part of the show," he says, nodding. "It makes you feel secure taking risks you wouldn't normally take. Maybe it starts with a little strangling and S&M. You have a false sense of security. You think we'll come if you need out. But one day we don't come, and things go too far."

"She's killing them?" I stare at Gabe and Mel. That can't be. I would have noticed if girls were disappearing. Wouldn't I?

"No. That's the thing—Black doesn't hurt the girls. She sends them out with a false expectation of safety. The client can pay to go as far as he wants—even if that means the girl will die."

The blood rushes from my face.

Mel interjects. "Those are the lucky ones, Avery. The transactions I was tracking—they weren't boxes of goods."

My stomach sinks. "Then what were they?"

"People. Girls. She sold them—alive, battered, and dead. In cages, crates, and cargo. She fucking sold them!" Mel's muscles tense and it looks like she wants to punch something.

Gabe keeps talking, explaining how it starts with something small, just what you're comfortable with. It's like a really good date. It might even be fun. Then it starts to slip into something else, but the girl stays. She says she's open to anything, and Black holds her to that. I hear Black's words rush through my mind.

I cut Gabe off. "She offered me a position as a madam."

"She had a buyer," Gabe says with a nod. "You narrowly avoided being sold."

Mel turns around and punches a box. The stack shakes but doesn't fall.

"That's what happened to my friend." Mel stares at the cardboard as she speaks. "She never came back, Avery, and Black wanted you for the same reason—you have that little bit of spunk, but it's not enough to save you. That's why she separated us. That's why she didn't choose me."

We're silent for a moment.

"You don't have anything to nail her with?"

"Nothing that will stick." Gabe's eyes fix on mine. "That's why I kept telling you to run. Once she has a buyer, the rest is a matter of time."

Swallowing hard, I ask the question even though I don't want to know the answer.

"Who's my buyer? Do we know?" Gabe sees where I'm going.

"It wasn't Sean if that's what you're asking."

I nod slowly. "Did he ever do something like that?"

Gabe shakes his head. "Not that I've seen. Sean Ferro is a calloused sonofabitch with a sordid history, but he didn't come around for other services. He was solely interested in you. The offer came from another account holder, one with a necrophilia request. Either way, your path with Black ends in a coffin."

## Chapter 5

I haven't slept for nearly a week. Every time I close my eyes, I dream of Sean. Our last few days play on a loop in my subconscious. I see his face, the hurt in his eyes, immediately followed by a double gunshot. I wake up covered in sweat, ready to scream. Heart pounding, I throw off the blankets.

Mel is sleeping across from me. She's got one eye open and her hand wrapped around a knife.

"Go back to sleep."

"I can't." Rubbing my face, I stretch and throw my legs over the side of the bed. "I keep seeing his face. The last things he heard weren't good." I get up and pull on a pair of jeans and throw my hair into a ponytail.

Mel groans and pulls the pillow over her head. "Not again."

"I need to run. I have to clear my head."

"You're trying to kill me." Mel throws her pillow and sits up. "We've slept for a total of five hours in four days, and you spend most of your awake time working out."

"So I don't flip out! Pick one, Mel, crazy Avery or buff Avery."

"Shoot me." Mel flops back on her bed.

We've been staying at Gabe's nephew's house on Long Island. He lives a few blocks from the cemetery where my parents rest. I pull a sweatshirt over my head and gesture for the knife.

"Just give it to me. I can go on a run and make it back fine."

"Really?" Mel arches a dark brow at me. "You've got not one but two psychos trying to find you, and today is the funeral of New York's most hated woman. You seriously expect me to let you go out alone?"

"No. I'm saying that I can go out alone. Whatever is going to happen, will happen anyway."

"Not while I'm there. Give me a minute."

"Yeah, sure." I don't want to argue with her. Since Mel told me about Miss Black's main business, she's had this haunted look in her eyes.

It's like she helped facilitate evil things and there's no way to wash the blood off her hands. Innocent women are gone, possibly dead, and she had a part in it. It's not her fault, but I understand her horror. I wonder what nefarious thing my actions set in motion.

The TV clicks on in the kitchen. Gabe's nephew is up and getting ready for work. The loudest news story all week has been about the body on the beach. They haven't released the name yet, but I already know who it is. I've tried to reach Peter and Jon, but they've gone dark. I haven't heard a peep from Marty or Trystan either.

"I can't wait anymore," I call out to Mel. "I'm going to lose it. I'll be out front."

"Fine, be right there." Mel is so grouchy.

I walk past our host. He's wearing a tattered red robe the color of dried blood. His hair is sticking up like he didn't sleep at all, and he's holding a newspaper in one hand and a steaming cup of coffee in the other.

"Morning."

"Hey, Avery. Is Mel going with you?" I nod. "I can wait with you until she gets ready." He drops his things and is ready to stand.

"I'll be right out front. Really, it's fine. You can see me through the window. I won't leave without her."

"Uncle Gabe will kick my ass if you do."

"I'm not leaving, Tim. I'll see you tonight. Maybe I'll cook something."

He laughs. I've been cooking non-stop since I got here. Tim's house is stuffed with lasagna, ziti, meatballs, and enough sauce to cause a tidal wave.

"Anything you want, Avery. Feel free to make pancakes."

"Yeah, you just don't want meatballs for breakfast."

"Does anyone?" Mel asks blurry-eyed from the doorway behind me. "Shit, I need coffee." She makes a beeline for the pot. "Go stretch. I'll be right there."

I nod. Mel isn't a morning person. "See you later, Tim." I push through the backdoor and start my day.

## Chapter 6

I'm pushing myself harder, trying to ignore the burn in my lungs and the pain in my side. I want to feel nothing. I want to feel numb from head to toe; my broken, dying heart reminds me of everything I've lost every time it beats. I can't face the world without him, I won't.

I'll never come to terms with losing Sean.

I'll never move on.

There are few people in my life that have left such a dramatic impression on me. For better or worse, and I prefer to think Sean was for the better, he pushed me, pulled me, and tried to meet me where I was. He tried to be what I needed. And failed. I failed.

I've lost everything and everyone dear to me.

The girl running at my heels is watching me, torn between two worlds. If Mel hands me over to Black, she'll be an instant millionaire—everything she ever wanted delivered on a silver platter. If she protects me, she gets nothing but honor. Honor doesn't buy much these days. I've slept with one eye open since she told me about what Black really does. Mel's confession should have convinced me she was on my side.

But it didn't.

It convinced me Gabe is truly a good guy, but it proved that I don't know Mel as well as I thought I did.

'Surviving justifies everything.' That's her mantra, her motto. So, why not trade me in for a new life? Her old life is worth peanuts in comparison.

Meanwhile, as I try to wrap my brain around that, I think about Black's empty promises. I wonder what she's set up and what would have happened if I'd said yes. Power, money, and everything I could possibly want—if I'd only do this one last thing? She was pushing me so hard to become a madam, but then what? What actually would have been the next step for me?

That's the trap. It's the way Black makes me feel empowered. She planted ideas in my head and I thought I could handle it. I wanted to handle it, but Sean made me back away. I wonder if he knew he was saving me. I wonder if he knew, in the end, he'd die because of me.

It's my fault his life ended violently.

It's my fault he never found peace.

NO.

I push harder, running ahead without waiting for Mel. I hear her gasping behind me.

"Fuck me sideways, Avery! It's uphill and 5 a.m. This bitch is gonna die. Slow the fuck down!"

But I don't. I push harder, faster, taking longer strides. My feet pound the pavement and it feels good. I want to hurt; I want the pain. It's the only way I can tell I'm still alive.

I stop short, horrified. Mel crashes into me and then collapses spread-eagle on the well-manicured lawn to my right. We're running in a subdivision that disguises the hell these people live through day in and day out. The pretty grass hides their dead souls, trapped in the constant craze of wanting more—of needing whatever's next.

I don't need anything. Except Sean.

And I thought he was messed up.

Without him, I'm doing the same thing—hurting myself to feel something. I'm walking the tightrope and know it's only a matter of time until I fall. I welcome the rush and crash of pain at the bottom. Bending at the waist, I grip my knees and try to catch my breath. I don't let Mel know what I was thinking.

"Get up," I huff, trying to straighten. A cramp pulls me back down, breathing like an overweight porn star.

Sucking. Air. Gonna. Pass. Out.

"I'm gonna roll over and rip up this guy's grass. Make it a blanket and go to sleep. It's so nice and cool under my gluteus maximus."

"You're such a dork," I say, laughing. "Say it like you mean it."

"The grass feels good on my ass!" Mel laughs and starts coughing.

"You should make that a thing and sell Sexy Sod on QVC. Only three easy payments of $19.95 and you, too, could have a sexy grassy ass."

"De nada."

Her sudden Spanish makes me laugh harder. The stitch in my side grows as I scold her. "I didn't say gracias! I said grassy ass! You giant dork!"

"You still laughed." Her smile fades as she stares at the early morning sky. "Did you ever think your life would come to this? I knew I was in for some messed up shit, but now I'm an informant to a fucking FBI agent."

I straighten and push my sweaty hair out of my face. "Yeah, every little girl dreams of being sucked into the sex industry when she's five. It's what we all strive for."

"I knew I'd have a rough life," Mel continues without laughing. "You can't torch your demons and, where I come from, demons never die. They're always there, trying to pull you back. I refuse to go back to that. That's my vice; that's my downfall."

We stay still and silent in the grass, watching the cars as they travel up and down the street. I notice a white van turn the corner and my stomach dips. It feels suspicious. Mel ignores it.

"It doesn't have to be. You choose what you do and who you'll be. Your past shapes you, but it can't hold you unless you let it."

Mel snorts. "So says the girl trying to induce a heart attack during a jog."

"Loss is different. It opens a hole into the soul letting anything rush in or out. Darkness and light collide together and life turns gray; grief isn't clearly defined."

"I know," Mel says carefully. "That's why I hope you'll forgive me."

Fuck. I dart upright and see the van parked a few doors down, idling. My eyes cut over to her.

"What'd you do?" I'm ready to run, but when I glance the other way, there's another car parked at the side of the street, waiting. "Mel. What'd you do?"

"Surviving justifies anything." Mel sits up and looks squarely into my eyes. "I just hope I did the right thing. Either way, it's too late to go back now."

Shit. I take off at a full run, wishing I hadn't pushed myself so hard. The van doors open and a few guys jump out the back. They're wearing polo shirts and khaki pants. What the fuck? I feel like the nerd crew from a techie store is chasing me. Glancing over my shoulder, I can see they're gaining. Their freaky-long limbs give them a huge advantage.

"Please," a speedy geek calls out to me, "wait a second!" He gasps and yells, "Miss Smith, please wait!"

At that name, every broken piece of my heart falls to the ground. My body freezes and my feet won't move. I'm standing in the middle of a tree-lined suburban street, gasping, too afraid to turn around. The one guy is close to me, but he doesn't come closer.

"Miss Smith, if you—"

"Don't," I snap. It's one word, a clear warning.

I'm going to lose it. No one calls me that— no one except Sean. The name does something to me. I can feel my sanity slip away and melt into hysteria. Sean is gone. These people are hoping to trap me with sweet pet names they overheard.

My fingers tap my hips anxiously, and I suck in the morning air, letting it fill my lungs. I feel a piece of me, something inside my brain—the part that holds back the crazy impulses—straining under the massive pressure. It's like a floodgate ready to burst. It can't hold the tidal wave of crazy back anymore.

I swear to God that I can hear it straining, creaking and cracking under the pressure.

"I'm sorry that I had to call you that, but you wouldn't have stopped otherwise." His voice is deep, sincere, and slightly winded.

CREAK.

"Go away. Leave me alone." I refuse to turn. Something is back there. They know something and I'm not going to make it through this. Whatever is in that van, I don't want to see it. Mel was muttering about choosing the right thing. I wonder if she knows how close I am to having a mental break down.

"I can't. I'm sorry, but I need you to come with me." He reaches his hand out toward me.

I stiffen and add another step between us. He drops back to his former position.

My stomach is in knots, twisting and turning, anticipating the horror that's to come.

If Sean's body is in there, if I have to see his dead body…

CRACK.

I visibly shiver, but I'm not cold. It feels like someone walked over my grave. It's the bone-chilling sensation that accompanies dread. It's flowing through me, freezing me from the inside out. My hands dart instinctively up to rub warmth back into my arms, but it doesn't help.

"There's no way in Hell I'm going with you." My voice is deeper this time, my eyes narrowed to slits, and I glance nervously over my shoulder. "Turn around and walk away."

The guy is young, possibly younger than me. That's weird. He doesn't look like the thug type. The guy next to him—a blonde with a goatee—reaches into his pocket. I round on them suddenly thinking he has a gun.

Goatee guy pulls a red piece of plastic from his pocket, shakes it, and pulls the cap off before sticking it in his mouth. He inhales sheepishly, takes the inhaler away from his lips, and smiles at me.

Asthmatic thugs. What the hell?

"Avery, please walk back with me. I'll tell the van to stay there." The leader resumes his negotiation.

"No way," I say, shaking my head and taking another step backward. "I won't willingly jump into the back of a windowless van. If Vic wants to talk to me, tell him to come over here." It has to be him. Or Black. It has to be someone Mel doesn't want to work with for her to say those things.

I glance around, looking for the traitor. She's gone. People suck.

The guys are glancing at each other. It seems like they don't know what to say. Goatee Guy steps toward me. I step back. He takes another baby step, speaking in a soothing voice.

"The thing is, it's not safe outside for either of you. If you'd come closer, you could see."

"Yeah right," I say with a bitter laugh. "I'm sure the inside of your kidnap mobile is filled with puppies, right? And candy? No, thank you. Keep driving, pervs."

"Do we look like henchmen?" Goatee Guy rolls his eyes and gestures to his companions. "Do you seriously think we're used to chasing strange women down the street and trying to get them into a van? We suck at it! This is our only attempt at this and you're not listening!" The guy seems ready to stomp his foot.

He lets out a sigh and pinches the bridge of his nose as he gestures with his other hand for his companions to flank me. They do, but by now I'm confident I could easily outrun them all.

"You're insane. Go get in your van and drive off a bridge. Leave me alone!" I'm yelling and stepping backward. I'm too loud. People are going to look.

Everyone realizes I'm going to take off at the same time. I whirl around and launch my body forward, and slam into a hard chest. One of the guys snuck up behind me. He wraps his arms around me, squeezing tight, but it's not a restraint—it's more of a hug. He buries his face in my hair and whispers in my ear.

"We have unfinished business, Miss Smith. Why do you always have to be such a pain in the ass?"

I pull back enough to see his face, but I already know who is holding me.

"Sean."

## Chapter 7

I lose it. Melting into his chest, I feel my knees buckle as my eyes overflow with tears.

"You... You're... I saw Vic shoot you."

Sean towers over me, holding me tight. He kisses my head several times, softly, carefully.

"He did. It grazed my side. He had other plans for me, but things didn't go well that day. For him." I pull back, look into his face and start bawling. I can't help it. Sean laughs lightly and pulls me closer to his chest. "It's good to know you care."

I slap his side, making him wince.

"Sorry, but you're an ass, you know that? Why'd you wait so long to find me?"

"Because, in case you didn't notice, you were hiding in this lovely neighborhood. If Mel hadn't gotten hold of me, I wouldn't have known you survived. I was sure Vic killed you. That guy is unhinged." Sean takes my face in his palms and holds me there. He gazes at me like he didn't expect to see me again.

"Is the baby all right?" His question cuts me to my core.

I start blubbering again and bury my face in his chest. Since he can't understand what I'm saying, he assumes the worst.

"You lost it? Avery, I'm so sorry. Oh, my God." He holds me gently, kissing the top of my head, and when I pull away to correct him, I see something that makes no sense. Sean blinks hard and swipes at his eyes. My jaw drops and I stare at him. Sean forces a smile.

"I know it wasn't mine, but I was happy for you. I could see you holding her in your arms. She was beautiful, just like you." He lifts his hand to my cheek, and I lean into his touch.

"Sean," I manage to choke out his name. I never expected him to be like this. I said the worst thing I could possibly think of to get him to leave me, and he's still here. He's crying over a baby I never had. I feel like an asshat. "It's not that. There was never a baby."

His expression shifts, becoming guarded once more. The vulnerability is sucked off his face and into the emotional black hole swirling within him. He's quiet, waiting for an explanation. I step away and twist my hands as I speak.

"I thought you were going to sacrifice yourself to save me. I couldn't stop you. No one can stop you when you're like that, Sean. I couldn't think of anything else that would throw you off, so I said I didn't love you. I added a fake baby when you wouldn't walk away. There was no baby and I don't love Trystan, not like that. I never have. It's always been you. I don't know how to get through this, but I can't lose you again." My lower lids come up as my vision goes blurry from unshed tears.

Sean is completely still. I have no idea what he's thinking. He doesn't even make an indication that he's heard me. He just stands in the middle of the street, staring blankly.

"Sean, say something." I try to catch his eye, but he doesn't move. "I was cruel and you should be pissed. Yell at me! Scream! I deserve it." As I say the last words, I press my hands to his chest and push.

Sean blinks and looks down at me. His hands cover mine. Those blue eyes pierce my soul and his beautiful face is a canvas of hope and adoration.

"When you said it was his, I realized something."

My heart slaps against my ribs, bursts through, and runs down the street. This can't be real. It can't be. He's going to say it; he's going to tell me he loves me. After denying it for so long, after continuously trying to push me away, he's going to say it. I can see it on his face.

"What?"

Sean presses his lips together and swallows hard. His lashes lower so that he's no longer looking me in the eye. Whatever he has to say is incredibly personal, so much so that he can't hide how vulnerable it makes him feel.

"I realized how badly I wanted a life with you—not the messed up version I thought we'd have, but a real life. Maybe it won't be in a Cape Cod house with a picket fence, but I saw us together on a couch with a baby on your lap. I saw you stroke her hair and kiss her cheek. I saw her pink dress and her little pink shoes. I saw her, Avery. She was the life we could have had. It wasn't the house or the fences. It wasn't about a dog or zip code. It was about us, about her. I wanted her so badly, and I never even realized it. A life with you would be complicated, but most dreams are—and I've treated you so badly—"

I press my fingers to his lips and stop him. Sean looks me in the eye.

"You want a baby?" He nods. "With me?" A smile lights up his face.

"Yes, with you. You're my home. I want to be wherever you are. If you'll have me, I want to build a life with you. I love you, Avery."

My lower lip begins to tremble and I can't stop it. Every emotion I've held in check for so long comes rushing out in the most ungodly sound. Sean's eyes sweep up to the guys, who have been watching us, and then back at me.

"Don't cry. We don't have to do anything. I shouldn't have said anything. I should have—"

I start laughing, which confuses him more. Sean's face is a mix of horror and bewilderment. I grab his face and kiss him, cutting off his words. When I pull back, I laugh again.

"I'm glad you did. I had no idea. None. This mess of tears and smiles is joy; I think you broke my face."

Sean smiles and pulls me to him. "You want me?"

"Always."

"You'll marry me? You'll be my wife?"

"And have your babies." I smile up at him. My gaze drifts to his lips and I really want to press my body against his and kiss him until I can't breathe.

Mel shouts from the back of the van. "Get your skinny asses in here! I knew this was stupid. It's got stupid white people written all over it. You two are brain dead!" Mel chucks something at us—a roll of tape—and it hits me in the shin before wobbling down the street.

"Fine." I take Sean's hand and start walking toward the vehicle. "I'll get in the van. But I know that tape was for me. You knew I wouldn't get in."

He squeezes my hand. "I knew you'd never give up."

## Chapter 8

*~Sean~*

I watch her like I'm in a dream and she may vanish. I thought I'd lost her—lost her heart to Trystan Scott and then her brother—I don't want to think about that. Vic Jr. is darkness, evil, worse than his father by far. Avery gazes over at me with those soft brown eyes. Her lips curve into a sweet smile.

"I can't believe you hired a geek crew and thought they could be ninjas. I bet kidnapping wasn't something they wanted on their resume."

Goatee Guy snorts. "True dat." He winks at me and makes a set of guns with his fingers, then tips them back and makes a "pfff" noise with his mouth.

"Justin," I say in a warning tone. The guy can't keep his mouth shut. The less Avery knows, the better. As it is, she's going to be pissed when she figures out who we're going to see.

"Sorry, boss." He leans back against the van wall.

Avery slips her small hand into mine, lacing our fingers together. She feels so good. I want to get her alone and trace every inch of her body with my hands. I want to feel her curves fill my palms, and watch as she presses into me. Memories of her flood my mind—her head tipped back, eyes closed, her long hair cascading down her back, and her perfect breasts are thrust forward. In my mind's eye, I see her in the shower in my rooms, dripping wet. Her body glistens under the spray of water as she leans against the cold tiles.

She's the sexiest woman I've ever met, willing to try anything, wanting to know what pleasures are to her liking—and mine. The most amusing part is that she has no idea how alluring she is, a siren in sneakers.

As I watch, her expression changes from contentment to inquisitiveness.

"What are you thinking about?"

I lean forward and touch her hair, pushing it away from those gorgeous eyes.

"Do you really want to know?"

She cocks her head to the side and adopts a stern look. "I wouldn't have asked if I didn't want to know. Tell me. You have a weird look on your face."

I lean in close to her ear, a breath away. She shivers, and I take the moment to tease her. "I've been thinking about how much fun it's going to be to make you my wife. In every sense of the word." My lips brush her ear before I pull away.

Her cheeks turn pink and she smiles shyly. That look makes me want her even more. Damn, she's beautiful!

I can't tell her exactly what I'm thinking; it's too much. The intensity of my feelings for her scares her. Fuck, it frightens me, too. Of course, it's too much, but love is like that. It comes in waves, and right now I'm at the crest. I want to breathe her in and feel her beneath me. I want her skin slick with sweat and writhing against me, crying out, calling my name and begging for release.

"Mr. Ferro," Bill says, handing me his phone. "He'd like to speak with you."

I swipe the phone from his hand. "What?"

"Where the hell are you? You were supposed to grab her and be here half an hour ago."

The guy is an asshole. There are people in the world that are born to be assholes. He is one of them. And he can't help it.

"We get there when we get there." I hit END CALL and hand Bill his phone.

"Where are we going?" Avery finally asks the question. She looks at the guys and when they don't answer, she takes my hand. A fake smile spreads across her lips. "I'm not going to like this, am I?" I shake my head. Hair falls into my eyes and I push it back.

"I'm afraid not. I know you're going to hate it, but it was a necessary evil. Do you remember Project 597?" The smile falls from her face and her back stiffens.

"You're not serious?" I don't reply. Avery's spine suddenly melts and she looks like a sulky teenager. I want to smile and pinch her face when she does that. It's a remnant of Avery from a more carefree time, from long before she met me. "Henry Thomas? You hate him."

"I do. Which makes him more predictable than anyone else. Henry will always do what serves his own best interest, which is why he fits perfectly into our plans."

She makes a face and then sits up straighter. With her hands on her knees, she looks over at me. "Spit it out, Ferro. How are we getting

Happy Hands to help? And does he know Mel is with us? She kicked his ass last time."

That makes me laugh. "No, he doesn't know Mel contacted me, but if she hadn't this plan wouldn't work. We have every piece we need to end this once and for all."

"What do you mean?"

"Vic Junior and his entire team will be wiped out, and Black will go down with them. After this is over, no one will ever come after a Ferro again."

## Chapter 9

*~Sean~*

Avery's voice is an octave too high. She yanks her hair out of her face and tosses it over her shoulder. Leaning in, she gets in my face. Her words come out in a rush, making the sentence sound like a single word. "AreYouInsaneWeCan'tBeHere!"

She's pissed.

We drive around Henry's South Shore estate to the back entrance of the mansion, where Justin parks the van in a garage that originally served as a stable. After purchasing the estate, Henry added wings onto the main house until it resembled one of England's Tudor palaces. He nurses an unhealthy infatuation with Henry

VIII. Both are rumored to have severe mood swings and teeter on the edge of crazy—maybe Thomas just views the former king as a kindred spirit.

Either way, Avery has every right to be appalled we're here. She's gone pale, the color washed from her cheeks since I said his name. She's shaking slightly. I take her hand in mine, but she pulls it away. "Avery, if we didn't need to be here, we wouldn't be. There's a reason for this. I promise."

"Do you know what he did to me?"

"I know and I'm sorry." My throat tightens. I dislike seeing her in this state.

"I thought you'd pick up the patent from him, not drive up to his freakin' house! How can you even trust him?" She pleads with me with those big brown eyes and I wish we could drive away, but it's not possible.

"I don't trust him. I don't trust anyone except you. If we could avoid this, I would."

Mel shoves past, elbowing me as she goes. She glares at me.

"This is a dumbass plan."

"You don't even know the plan," I snap.

"Yeah, that's why it's stupid. If Mr. British tries any shit, I'll make good on my former threats." Mel opens the door of the van and jumps out.

Henry Thomas is standing there. He's dressed in a pair of slacks and an angora sweater. Coupled with loafers and a turtleneck, he looks like he belongs in a magazine, not planning nefarious things to end the Campone family's reign in New York.

"Oh, dear God." He flinches when he sees Mel. "You brought the beast along?" Mel lowers her hood, walks over to him, and gets up in his face. Henry doesn't back down. Spine straight, the two of them are nose to nose.

"Funny, I said the same thing about you. Just because you dress all proper and shit doesn't make you any less of a freak." She flicks the collar of his turtleneck.

He laughs lightly, acting like her words don't bother him. His pupils darken and grow wider. He likes her that close. The woman is beautiful and dangerous.

"No, my dear, you are as freaky as they come."

Mel opens her mouth to let him have it, but I cut her off.

"Drop it. Whatever you two want to dish out has to wait. We have a limited amount of time."

Henry steps back, lifting one brow at me. His arms are folded over his chest.

"Very well. Another time, fair maiden." The last two words drip with sarcasm.

"Assface," Mel mutters in reply.

We're still standing in the garage. The chauffeur isn't around. Henry's eyes sweep over Avery as she climbs out, his jaw clenching tightly. I step between them. I'm not entirely certain what transpired between them, but Henry isn't the type to forgive and forget. Odds are, he's still livid.

"Show me what you've done with the project," I say, redirecting his attention to me. Henry presses his lips together tightly and nods.

"Follow me."

We walk out of the garage and follow a path around to the back of the house. We enter a room filled with floor to ceiling panes of glass decorated with wrought iron scrolling. Each pane looks like hand-blown glass. It's a statement, a claim to having more money than God, and too ostentatious for my taste. We enter through an elaborately decorated iron door. Henry gallantly holds it open for Avery and Mel to pass through. As Avery passes him, she looks back at me, worry clearly visible in her eyes. I steel myself. If I don't, I won't be able to follow through with this plan.

That's what concerns me most. Avery will see the way I think, the way my mind can devise a cruel plan to painfully destroy my enemies. I can't hold back or it won't work. That's been my vice in the past—trying to do things within the parameters of mercy. Vic Jr. is beyond mercy. He views compassion as weakness. He showed my mother no mercy and will receive no mercy in return.

Justin follows behind us and, once inside, remains by the door. Avery leans in close to me and takes my hand.

"I don't like this."

I kiss her temple and release her fingers. I don't respond because there's nothing to say. I don't like this either, but it's necessary.

Henry pads across ornate rugs and around velvet couches, to an antique desk large enough to sleep on. A carved stone mantle frames the massive desk, stretching the length of two men at least. Henry sees me looking at it, smiles, and strokes the carved details appreciatively.

"Imported from England. It was salvaged from an estate belonging to the Duke of Suffolk during the reign of King Henry VIII. It's quite charming."

Mel laughs. "Charming? What the fuck is wrong with you? Your fireplace is bigger than my dorm room. There ain't anything charming about that shit. Nah, you're overcompensating for something." Mel smirks. "Is your dick smaller than you'd like?"

Henry stops smiling and walks toward her.

"There's nothing small about me, miss. Isn't that right, Avery?"

Avery's spine goes ramrod straight. Mel starts to speak, but I talk over her.

"Enough! We don't have the luxury of squabbling or wasting time. As it is, we're down to the wire. It's a game and this is our last move."

"Your last move, not mine." The pride in Henry's voice is more than I can handle.

"That's where you're wrong. You've been on Vic's list for ages. He hasn't bothered to take you out because you were giving his dad a reason to keep you alive. Vic Jr. doesn't give second chances. As soon as he finds out you and I were together—and he will—you'll die in a very unpleasant way."

Henry sneers. "Then why should I help you?"

"Because I have something you need." I pause a moment and tell him. "Campone's ledgers point to a series of unsavory transactions that involve the purchase of this property."

"My father bought this property," Henry begins proudly, his back stiffening, "along with most of the land in this area."

"Which is exactly why you wouldn't want these ledgers leaked. I'm certain that you are aware of how this land was acquired and what will happen if the district attorney were made aware of the situation." Henry doesn't move. His eyes get a vacant blank stare, which tells me his mind is reeling, trying to find a way out—but there isn't one. I've got him by the balls and he knows it.

Finally, he nods. "But if you fail, I die. Vic will know I was involved. As it is, I'm having difficulty shaking that little shit."

"That's why I came to you. I know you'll want to eliminate any pertinent threats and, now that he's blown up mine, Vic will be on your doorstep next. This is a preemptive move for you. Since you've been playing nice, he won't see it coming."

Henry sits down behind his desk and leans back into his chair, tapping his fingertips together. I remain standing, my arms folded across my chest.

Mel flops on a couch and lets out a howl.

"Holy mother of—what the hell is this made of? Bricks?" She rights herself and rubs her elbow.

Henry looks over at her, then Avery, who is sitting on the arm of a couch. "I prefer my things hard."

"Like your head."

"Among other things," Henry says with a smirk before returning his gaze to me. "I'm inclined to agree with you, especially since he already managed to remove the matriarch of your family." The bastard sits there, audaciously smiling over the death of my mother and the loss of our home. "Project 597 was the prototype. I combined the patent I bought from you with hardware I already had, to create something of a marvel. Unfortunately, I haven't been able to profit from it yet. They need a test run."

"You already have a buyer?" I know he does, and I know who the buyer is, but I want to hear what he has to say about it.

"I do," he says, nodding proudly. "However, we're at an impasse until I prove Project 597 is in working order."

Avery speaks up. "What are you talking about?"

She was there when Henry bought the patent, but she didn't know what he planned to do with it. I didn't think he'd get it working, but he did.

Henry smiles at her. The way his eyes sweep over Avery makes me want to punch him in the face. He remembers something, something sexual. I bury the impulse to throw him through the wall.

"Project 597 is a chaos device." He opens the top desk drawer and pulls out a small box. As he speaks, he opens the lid and takes out a small black bead. "It boasts many marvels, but in this case it functions as an anti-security device. You could compare it to a magnet on a hard drive."

Mel asks, "It fucks stuff up?"

"In a manner of speaking, yes. It renders computers useless. Sean's patented material combined with my technology made it possible. And the best part is no one will notice a thing until it's too late. Unlike other devices that disable cameras, computers, and locks—this one successfully tricks the security programs— allowing one to move through a system undetected. If you shut a security system off completely, the computer alerts the owner and authorities."

Mel asks, "So why won't this trip the alarm?"

He glances over at her. "Simple. It's because the computer thinks it is still running. The cameras will begin to play backward, so it doesn't appear frozen. This device alters the timestamp and initiates the pause by proximity."

"So this has to be near the main computer system Vic uses?" Avery stares at the little black bead and swallows hard. She knows what's coming, what I'm going to have her do.

"It does, which is why it's housed in this cute little contraption." Henry holds up the bead in the light.

"Add a gold chain and that looks like Black's bracelet." Mel realizes the plan as she says it. "Aw, shit! You're sending us in? That's the plan. Avery and I sneak in, then you guys kill everyone?"

Henry laughs and holds up his hands. "I'm not killing anyone. In fact, I'm not going."

"Can't get that sweater dirty, huh?" Mel's gaze narrows while she looks at Henry. When she turns to me, she's all business. "What's the plan, Ferro? All of it—spill!"

"Black will get an order she can't refuse. Avery will walk right into the trap, and she'll be sent to Vic. He's been wanting her and knows Black can't say no. Black has been doing everything within her power to get Avery to say yes, so go in and agree. Wear your bracelet like you always do and we'll know where you are. Vic is going to take you to his house. He'll want to boast before he does anything and show you what he took from you. Before he can do anything, I'll come for you. Then we'll show him how it feels to see his home explode. He'll get to watch from the inside."

"Sean," Avery's voice is weak. Her jaw is hanging open. "How do you know he'll take me there? What if he goes somewhere else?"

I cross the room to her. Mel moves and I take her seat on the couch next to Avery.

"You don't have to be the one to go in, but if you do, it'll be less obvious that we've got him. He won't know we're there until it's too late. The fact that he kept you alive says a lot. Vic hates you. He won't just shoot you. That'll end too fast."

"What if something goes wrong? What if you can't get to me in time?" Avery's skin is becoming paler, glistening. Her breathing is quickening, and when she takes my hand, she holds it tighter and tighter. I wish we didn't have to do this, but we have to.

"I will. I'll get to you. And if something goes wrong, Mel will be there."

Her eyes meet mine and hold. Fear is overflowing, but she just nods.

"Sean, you know why he wants her, right?" Mel sounds uneasy. Her voice is tight and she's lost her normal carefree vibe. "Vic is well beyond being a perv."

"I know."

"He wants to have sex with his sister... after he kills her."

Henry chokes suddenly and stands up.

"What? How do you know that?"

"He's been asking for her, you're right," Mel says, glancing briefly at Avery and then back at me. "He didn't say exactly what he wanted to do, but it just clicked. He wants someone he can't have—Black puts a higher price on that. Avery's his half-sister. Then it falls under the other contract with the crazy high fees because Black is kidnapping someone for him. Black asked him if this was a reorder, but he said he wanted something different. The other women vanished, no bodies, but the last two—they turned up."

"What are you saying?" Henry places his hands on the desk and leans forward. "That he's killing these women?"

"Yes but, more than that, I think he's crossed the line."

"Yeah, well, wanting to bang his sister proved that point."

"You're thinking something else," I say, prompting her to continue.

"I'll find out for certain if we go through with this. It'll show up." Mel stops talking and paces the room. She's never this quiet. I know what she's thinking, but Avery and Henry don't.

"You can't stop there!" Henry looks at me and realizes that I already know. "What does he want with her?"

"Let her confirm the order when they go to Black's office. It'll tell us how much time we have. Mel, can you tell Gabe we're coming? We'll need him out of the way to take out Black."

"Done," she says, nodding. "What about Black? You're going to lure her there?"

"Black will want to gloat," I begin slowly. "She's been jealous of Avery from day one. I'm sure you noticed the way Black was behaving around you?" I take Avery's hand. "She wanted to break us apart, and I now believe it had more to do with our past relationship than I originally thought. I didn't love her, but it's clear how I feel about you."

Mel starts to mutter something, but Avery glares at her. Mel swallows her words and turns toward Henry, wide-eyed without comment. Henry smirks.

"Can you two give us a moment?" Avery's voice is strong again, certain. Henry rolls his eyes, but grants her request.

"After you, my lady." He bows in front of Mel.

"Don't make me kick your ass in your own home," she snaps. "That'd be embarrassing."

The two exchange quips all the way into the hallway, and it's not until the heavy wooden door closes behind them that the sound completely fades.

"Sean, do you really think this will work?" Her brows wrinkle together as she watches me, worrying.

"I do." I take her hands in mine and rub the back of her hand with my thumb. "In the past, I've held back. I haven't used every resource available to me. I've tried to shield you and keep you out of it, but they won't leave you alone. Not now, not ever. This is a plan he won't see coming. He already knows Black has been trying to get you to agree. Black is a patient woman. This has been in the making for months and we'll use it against her. Ultimately, it'll cause her downfall."

"She still loves you, doesn't she?"

I close my eyes and look away. Shaking my head, I tell her the truth.

"I don't know if she ever loved me. I think she just enjoyed the concept of being a Ferro. She chose her life and I chose mine. She thought I was unattainable, but then you caught me. Jealousy rears up for many reasons. We're going to use that to our advantage."

She squeezes my hands and looks up at me.

"And Henry? You really think he won't screw us over?"

"It won't get that far. I plan on doing a test run before I send you out with it. Mel will have a second bead as well. I'm hoping Black will offer to accompany you two. Gabe said he'll be ordered to drive you to a location and Mel will follow to close the deal. The exchange is done onsite."

"How much money are we talking about? It seems like a weird question, but I was wondering..." her voice trails off.

"You're wondering how much you're worth? Avery, that's not an indication of anything except hatred."

"Five figures? The same amount you paid?" She looks up at me and pleads with those sexy eyes.

"Fuck, Avery." I run my hands through my hair and push off the couch. Walking away from her, I say, "I'd give everything I have to keep you out of this."

"I know you would." She gets up and walks over to me. She splays her fingers across my chest and takes my face in her hand. She turns my chin until I'm looking her in the eye. Her scent fills my head and I want to pull her against me and never let go. "And I know you don't like talking about how we got together."

"I returned you."

"Yeah, that." She smiles. "I'm just glad things turned out this way. I keep wondering if I'd do it again, and I want to think I wouldn't—but if that means losing you—I couldn't walk away. I love you, Sean."

"I love you, too." I pull her into my chest and feel her breasts press against me as her arms lace behind my back. "We have a few hours before everything is ready tomorrow morning. I'd like to spend that time with you, doing things that make you squee and go cray-cray."

She giggles against me and I can't keep the smile off my face. "When you put it like that, how can I say no?"

**Chapter 10**

*~Sean~*

Henry gives us a guest room and leaves quickly. It's midday and the sunlight cuts through the windows forming shafts of light on the rugs. Fresh clothing lays on the canopy bed. The room is dressed in reds and golds. I notice a plaque with a unicorn and a lion on the wall above the fireplace. It's as if the room is in a time warp.

"He has a bit of a fetish with old crap, doesn't he?" Avery glances around, lips parted.

"Circa 1500 or so, yes, and he's proud of his period pieces. It wouldn't surprise me if the window panes downstairs are original to that duke's home that he looted." I walk through the room and look into the bath. It's European style, too, with a basic shower minus the curtain, and massive claw-foot tub.

"I would have never thought he'd like this stuff," Avery says, laughing to herself. "He seems so cutting edge. I thought he'd have a robot staff and moving sidewalks in his super-modern house. Not a relic from the old country."

Sean shrugs. "To each his own. What do you want our house to look like? Modern? Country?" She sticks out her tongue at me. "What, you don't like shabby chic?"

Avery walks over to me and pushes me on my shoulders. The bed is a step behind me. I step back and then she shoves me again.

"Sit, Mr. Jones." She shoves me hard and I fall back on the massive bed. Avery grins and pushes me back onto the bed as she straddles my lap. My response to her begins to strain against my jeans. She smiles when she feels me reacting to her. I reach for her waist and rest my hands on the curve of her hips.

"I know, French modern."

"Maybe." She smiles at me and nods slowly. "Or Tuscan with an Avery flare."

"An Avery flare? Is that code for glitter?"

"You know me so well." She laughs. The sound is rich, so filled with joy it makes me want to hear it again. Her laughter is like food for my soul. I can never have enough.

I'm pulled from my thoughts when her smile fades and her gaze locks on my mouth. She sits there, above me, looking down at me like an angel. Her dark hair falls over her shoulders as she leans forward. Slowly, she inches toward me and her lips part slightly.

She stops just above my mouth and brushes her breasts against me ever so slightly. The sensation is all consuming. The lightness of the touch makes me want it even more. I slip my hands up her back to pull her down, trying to feel those perfect curves press against my chest, but she remains where she is, just above me.

"Do you trust me, Sean?" The way she says it makes my stomach flutter. It's as if she wants to torment me with light kisses and thinks asking my permission will make me say yes.

She must read my mind, because she quickly adds, "I've been thinking about things, things that terrify both of us, and I want to see if there's middle ground."

"There's not." I push up on my elbows, but she swats my shoulder and pushes me back into the bed. I try not to smile at her even though I want to.

There's something about Avery that ignites everything I've attempted to repress deep within me—no, it was beyond that. I didn't repress my emotions, my feelings that lead to joy, happiness, or hope. I destroyed them.

All this time, my face has been devoid of emotion. No one can read me, ever. I don't allow it. My heart isn't on my sleeve—it's been decimated by my own hand. There's been no trace of emotion left within me, and yet—this damaged, beautifully broken woman found a speck of hope, a remnant of the man I once was. She could have used it against me. I wouldn't have seen it coming. For all I knew, I was barren and utterly broken. She took that scrap of a soul, as she calls it, and nurtured it.

Now it wants to grow and will flourish if I let it. The thing is, it's been so long since I trusted anyone that I struggle not to maintain my old ways. So when she says something that makes me want to smile, I don't. When she does something that makes me want to laugh, I swallow that joy and banish it from my face.

My emotions have rooted within me once again and are dying to burst free. I feel the need to laugh tickle me from within, and it's getting harder to hide the joy she brings. These things have the power to destroy me. I've perfected the art of living alone and needing no one. I'm self-sufficient in every sense of the word. That ability made it possible to erect walls thicker than any vault. They were impenetrable, indestructible, but Avery floated through, like a ghost, aimed directly for my heart. I was too shocked to run, too elated to remain alone.

I can push her away, I can protect myself, but at some point she might not come back. Life without Avery would be unbearable. I can't fathom it.

There's one thing that frightens me as much as it exhilarates me. She senses it. I know she does. It's beyond skin on skin or pretty words that fade after fucking someone who doesn't matter.

Avery matters.

Avery knows she matters.

That's the bridge we have to cross. There's no way Avery will allow us to stay on the safe side of our emotions, half alive and hiding behind walls of our own making. I press my lips together and try to relax, but I can feel the nerve in my jaw twitching. It wants to take action, contort my face to a scowl, and silence my words. The fastest way to pierce a heart is with indifference. Stubborn urges rise up within me, making me want to lash out and run.

No one has ever terrified me more.

No one has seen what she sees in me. Avery perceives a good man, a man I once strove to be but abandoned. Truth be told, I wonder if that version of me would have been more successful in love and in life. I thought his heart was a weakness, something that would lead to his demise. I murdered him long before I lost Amanda. I destroyed him before anyone else could.

I'm so distant from my thoughts I don't even call that young man me. I say him because it feels less personal. It makes his mistakes sting less. It divides my life in a way that creates a dichotomy of weakness and strength. Things Sean could do and things he could not. There is nothing else.

Until I met Avery.

The good man I was once cried out from the wasteland that was once my soul, begging me to hold on to her. I know she's my last chance at…life, love, everything.

The human being I've become is not who I strove to be. When I was a boy I wanted power, but I also wanted grace. I wanted to be compassionate and trustworthy. I didn't want to resemble my father in any shape or form. When I surpassed his callousness, his cruelty, I remember understanding him for the first time. It made me think this path was walked for a reason. I saw why Ferro men cling to this path, this attitude, this life.

It's difficult to admit the enormousness of my mistake, but I no longer wish to remain on this path. The only way to fix this is through her—through Avery. I know she's my only chance. She's compassionate where I am calloused, hopeful where I am cynical. She has more to be afraid of from life than I can fathom, and yet—here she is, with me.

Is it a change in the truest sense of the word, to revert to a previous version of you? How hard will it be to find myself amongst the ashes and carnage that I've left in my wake all these years?

Will she run when she realizes this part of me will always be with me, trying to pull me back into darkness? That I'll never feel good enough, strong enough, or tough enough to help her endure the storms life throws our way?

She watches me, her gaze intensely focused on my eyes, waiting for an answer. It's hard to watch her and not feel anything. I can't begin to fathom the emotions bubbling up from inside me. I once thought she poked a hole in a dried-up river bed within me, but it was so much more than that.

She broke my walls and let the water from within the damn flow free. She saw the impending deluge and she didn't run.

She's still here.

She chose me.

"We don't know that. There might be a place in the middle. There's something we haven't really done, and I'm not asking you again. Do you trust me?" Avery looms over me with those deep brown eyes, her lips pulling into a sexy smile. She shifts her weight and rubs against me, making me moan. The tension between us is growing larger by the moment.

I'd planned on taking her up here and kissing her—doing soft things that she enjoys—but I'm not sure what to make of this request. It reminds me of our time in the hospital, and I'm curious.

She sweeps her body over mine, barely touching, and whispers in my ear, "Trust me."

Shivers erupt over my skin as her words consume me. The haunting way she says it, the way she changes her question to a command, undoes me. I relax into the bed and take a deep breath. Her eyes flick to my lips. When she looks up, she silently demands my answer.

I can barely breathe. The air is too hot and there's not enough to fill my lungs. I hide what she does to me, as my mind insists on taking small breaths, not giving away how much I want her—how much I need to be inside her. I fight against mental restraints cultivated in a lifetime of pain.

I suck in a shaky breath as a tremor rips through me. "I trust you. Completely."

## Chapter 11

*~Avery~*

I lean over him, waiting. I can see he's fighting something in his mind. I don't know what it is or why this is so hard for him. I wish I knew the exact reason and can only hope that one day, he'll tell me.

I push the thought away. I don't want to focus on tomorrow right now. I don't want to think about what might happen to us if we fail. I know this may be the last time we're together, and if things go to Hell—I know I won't see him again. I know my fate. I have my plan B, which Mel grudgingly accepted and then helped me perfect. Either way, Vic Jr. isn't going to live past tomorrow.

I don't have the same certainty—one way or the other—for Sean or for me.

I want this to be something we both enjoy—something that's freeing, exhilarating, and perfect. Not because my hips are in perfect proportion to my ass, but because he loves me and I love him. I watch him shiver after he speaks and I can't help but smile. He's fighting the walls that normally come up now, when he's most vulnerable. Which leaves me with a very raw version of Sean, one I've rarely seen. I trace the pads of my fingers along his cheek and then up into his hair, pushing it away from those crystal eyes.

"Let go. Release your thoughts." I kiss his temple and lean back slightly, enough to see his face. "Let go of your fears. It's just us. I won't hurt you." Leaning in, I kiss his other temple and hear his breath catch in his throat.

His voice is a whisper, "I know you won't." It seems like he wants to say more, but his jaw tenses and he stops speaking.

I place my fingers on his face and slide them over the stubble on his chin, and down his neck, across the soft spot on his throat, and down to his chest. My gaze follows my hand, except for the occasional glance at Sean's face. I wish I could watch his eyes through this whole thing, but I want to focus on touching him as well.

When I glance at him, his eyes are closed and his chin tips up. The muscles in his arms are corded tight like he's trying to break free from invisible bindings.

Leaning in, I press my lips to his throat. Sean sucks in hard, one gasp. The warmth of my mouth feels good against his skin. I slide my lips down and kiss a lower place, the one right above his Adam's apple. I feel him swallow hard and take a short breath before I dip lower. His hands pull at the sheets and I know how intense this feels for him. It feels that way for me, too.

Sean Ferro has protected his life and his heart from everyone. He's let me kiss the sides of his neck, but not here—not this soft spot that's completely unguarded—and not his chest. It makes him feel vulnerable, something Sean can't compartmentalize his way around.

But it's different now. He allows me to kiss him, not hiding the effect I'm having. Normally he shuts that down, but not now.

I slip my lips to the soft spot at the base of his neck and slide my tongue along his skin. The motion makes him inhale, and his chest rises, pressing into mine. He holds onto the sheets tighter and presses his hips to mine, making it impossible not to feel how turned on he is. Sean's eyes are shut tight, but his lips part and he moans my name, "Avery."

I press another kiss to that sensitive spot, sending a shiver through his body. His hands dart up and take hold of my shoulders tightly. His eyes fly open and he's panicked, staring at me, breathing like there's not enough air for the two of us.

"Please…" he says the word and releases my arms, letting his hands drop to my hips. He holds onto my thighs tightly and pulls down, pressing my core against him.

"No." I say the word gently. His blue gaze flicks up to my eyes and holds. He's ready to run, I can see it on his face. This pushes him into a place he's afraid to go.

I sit up completely, arching my back before pulling my shirt over my head. I toss it to the floor and unhook my bra. Pressing my lips together, I allow the fabric to dangle off my finger before dropping it on the bed. His eyes sweep over me, taking in my curves and fixating on the place where my bra had been. I smile down at him.

"It's hard to be on the bottom. Isn't it?" I wiggle my hips as I say it, making my horrible pun clear.

Sean barks an unexpected laugh. "Breaking the tension, are we?"

"Maybe. You look a little freaked."

"Maybe I am."

"Maybe I want you to be. Maybe we're both control freaks, and maybe it's nice to give someone else control once in a while." He watches me for a moment, hesitant to agree.

"Nice isn't a word that goes with sex. Nice is something that's barely adequate. It's not special. It's not extrordinanary—it's just nice."

I roll my eyes and stand up on the bed, one foot on each side of his hips. I slip off my panties and kick them into the air. They hit the wall and fall down behind a dresser. I stay like that, laughing over him. "How's the view from down there?"

Sean laughs—no, it's more of a giggle—and grins widely.

"Nice."

"If I couldn't distinguish your sarcasm, Mr. Jones, that would have gotten you in trouble."

"Oh, are you dishing out punishments? Perhaps I should be a bit of an asshat, you know, just to see what you'll do."

The banter is light and flirty. I love it.

"Shut up, chatterbox."

"You'll have to make me, Miss Smith. There's not much you can do that will render me speechless at this point, so..." Sean's words die in his mouth as I step over his shoulders and sit down slowly, lowering myself onto his lips. I'm straddling his face, offering my most sensitive parts for him to devour. My heart is pounding as the initial contact changes to something more.

I hear him moan beneath me and then his lips part. His hands come up and brace my hips as his tongue sweeps between my seams. The movement is so sudden and so deep that I'm caught off guard. I lean forward and press my palms against the wall, bracing myself. The one kiss sends shockwaves through me that travel the entire length of my body.

This isn't a starting point and I wasn't really ready for it, but I wanted to wipe that smug look off his face. His tongue moves against me again, licking me as deeply as possible. I gasp and resist the urge to rock against him.

In a teasing voice I say, "You'll have to do better than that, Mr. Jones, if you want me to—"

My words trail off abruptly as his tongue pushes inside me. Sean grips my hips harder and pulls me down on his face. I gasp and clutch the wall, trying not to melt and fall backward. Being upright makes everything feel different. My body is tingling and with every move of his lips against me, I want more. Moaning, I start to rock against him.

Sean encourages the movement. His mouth presses harder against me, making me want more. My breasts ache, wanting to be touched so badly that I hold them tight, continuing the slow build. Sean's kisses are relentless, pressing deeper, flicking the right places, and making me cry out. I want to come against his mouth and can no longer control my hips. They want to buck against him, forcing him in deeper, feeling his kisses; his hot mouth against me is too much. Sean holds onto my hips and keeps me still. I can't rock against him. I'm so close. His tongue is just below the spot that I need.

"Sean, please," I moan.

But he holds me still, not allowing me to move against him. His kisses change from slow and leisurely to desperately hungry. I cry out and fall forward, clutching the wall. His tongue flicks against the perfect place before pushing deep inside of me. Sean repeats the movement again and again, tugging my hips down hard every time his tongue presses into me.

The sensation is all consuming. I can't think. I can't move. My thighs are trembling and unable to hold this position for much longer. I feel his mouth work against me and the tightness that forms deep within me suddenly explodes into intense waves of pleasure. I scream his name and buck wildly against his mouth, enjoying every second of it.

When the waves die down, I slide down his chest and press my body against his. Sean smells like me. It makes me grin like a schoolgirl. He kisses my temple and pulls my hair back so he can see me. Our bodies are slick with sweat and Sean's heart is still racing in his chest. I can feel the rapid beating beneath me.

"Will you always silence me like that? If so, I approve."

I laugh and take his face in my hand, pulling it toward me. "Only when you're moderately bad. I have other plans for when you're really naughty."

Sean's lips pull up into a grin. "Really? You've been planning this?"

"More daydreaming than planning, but yeah. And thank you. I wasn't sure about it."

Sean's finger is tracing an invisible circle on my arm. "I'm glad you did."

We lay there in comfortable silence for a while. I finally ask him, "What are you thinking about?"

"You. I'm thinking that we should get married tonight."

I dart upright. One of my breasts was plastered to his chest and stings, but shock overwhelms me.

"What?" When Sean's only response is a soft smile, I blink at him. "Are you serious?"

"Of course. When am I not serious?"

"Pretty much never."

"I want to marry you, Avery. I have no idea how tomorrow is going to turn out, and I'd regret not taking that step with you. We've been tossed all over the place, and our lives have been out of control lately. But this—we can choose this—we can do it now if you'll have me." His voice is tight with worry. Sean presses his lips together, watching me.

I imagined being his fiancée and then beyond that—having the little house and maybe even being Mr. Turkey's sister-in-law—but I never pictured the actual wedding. It was a sore spot, a place I couldn't see. My father isn't here to walk me down the aisle. My mother isn't alive to help me get ready. I'm alone.

"So, we'd elope?"

He nods. His hopeful blue gaze locks on mine. Sean remains still, laying on the comforter with his head on a pile of fluffy pillows. The sunlight changes from bright white to golden oranges. Night is falling. We could be married tonight; we could be married right now. All I have to do is say yes.

Sean watches me, hopeful. His breathing is slow and his lips are parted as if he wants to say more. He finally sees our life together. He wants me, and not just for now, but forever. When he said he saw me holding a baby girl, I realized how much I wanted that, too. It's the future I couldn't have. Sean said he wasn't that guy, but he's changed. And so have I.

Watching Sean, I make my decision.

Turn the page for an excerpt from:

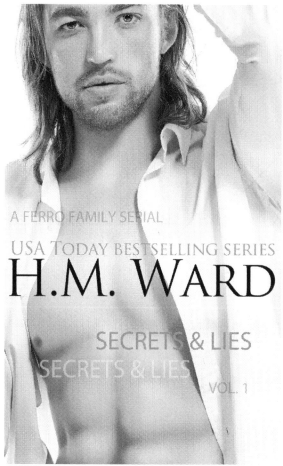

A FERRO FAMILY SERIAL

USA TODAY BESTSELLING SERIES

H.M. WARD

SECRETS & LIES

SECRETS & LIES

VOL. 1

SECRETS & LIES, Vol. 1
by H.M. Ward

## Chapter 1

Is he serious? What an assface! I stumble through the quad, accidentally bumping shoulders with someone.

"Watch it, bitch." I look up to see a pointy-nosed girl surrounded by a pack of nasty friends, all sneering at me. I have no friends here, not yet.

The truth is, my life sucks. It's sucktacularly fucked up and I refuse to cry on the first day of college, but I'm having trouble swallowing the plate of shit my wonderful boyfriend just force-fed me. Excuse me, force-texted me. The asswipe texted me. He didn't even call. The more I think about it, the more my throat tightens. Breathing is overrated.

I mumble, "Sorry," and get the hell out of there, before they hogtie my ass and toss me down a flight of stairs. Not that I've ever seen anyone hogtied, but this is Texas, right? I'm out of my element, by far.

As I hurry away, I hear my roommate's voice ring out, "That's right, Bacon! You better run!" The girls all giggle like Chelsey just said the funniest thing they've ever heard. Great. She's leader of the bitch pack. Why can't I ever attract a psycho sans backup? My luck sucks. Have I said that? Well, bad luck is my key feature and the bane of my existence.

As I haul ass across the quad, my phone chirps. Don't look at the screen. Don't look at it! I chant to myself, but I can't. I have to see what he said. It might be an apology. He might be breaking up with his other girlfriend and texted me by accident. Uh, wait. That'd be worse. I think.

The thing is, we've been together since we were kids. Our parents used to joke that we'd be married one day, as if it were meant to be. It even felt like fate brought us together. On the day we met, I was playing outside when a terrified bunny chased Matt the two blocks from his house to my front yard. Running blindly, Matt mowed me down, leaving me for the bunny to attack instead of him.

Okay, this bunny was the size of a small dog and had a hunger for marigolds. In an effort to save their gardens from becoming rabbit food, the sweet little old ladies in the neighborhood were actively trying to poison it. I saved that rabbit from the wrath of the grannies and my prize was Matt. He called me cool names like Rabbit Slayer. Okay, it sounded cool in grade school, and much better than the normal nicknames kids give each other. Boogerface or Rabbit Slayer? Please. Like that's even a choice.

Matt and I have been together so long, I've forgotten what it feels like to be apart. Now the unthinkable has happened and I'm two thousand miles from home, completely on my own. Matt is everything to me.

I pluck the phone from my pocket and scan the screen.

There's this other thing…

Fuck. Like it could get worse. He already broke up with me. What's worse than that?

I type back, I doubt it.

No, you need to know. There's someone else. I'm in love with her, Kerry.

The prickling sensation hits the back of my eyes hard and fast. As I push through the door, I turn right and search for a bathroom. I can't fake my way through this. I can't sit here and pretend that he didn't just rip my heart out.

How can there be someone else? I was his and he was mine. We were a couple. I have his damned ring on my finger. We were going to give this long distance relationship thing a chance.

But Matt didn't give it a chance.

A sob escapes my throat and my vision blurs. I race down the hallway, feeling the stares of strangers following in my wake. I can't cry now. I'm trying so hard not to, but my heart won't listen. It's curling into a ball and shriveling inside my chest. Grief takes hold of me, but I'm not crying yet. I try to find a restroom, holding back the cascade of sorrow that's building behind my eyes.

Plowing through the door, I head straight for the mirrors. There are always sinks by mirrors. I slam my books down on the counter and clutch the edge of the sink. Big gasping sobs wrack my body as I bend over the sink and stare at the white basin. Just as my tears start to fall, I see something move in the mirror. I feel eyes on me and the hairs on the back of my neck stand on end. I hadn't noticed anyone—not that I could see with my eyes full of tears.

Glancing up, I look across the room and don't understand what I'm looking at. A guy is standing by the wall. He's tall and toned, with dark hair and of standard build. At least, that's what he looks like through tears. Why is he in the girl's room? My brain is broken. I stand there and gape, not realizing that he's holding his thingy in his hand and standing in front of a urinal.

A crooked smile lines his lips when he sees me staring. "I, uh, think you're turned around."

His voice doesn't reach me. My body is in the middle of a full-fledged freak out and there's a guy in the ladies room, peeing on the wall. What the hell kind of school is this? I keep blinking, but I can't wrap my brain around what I'm seeing.

I manage to squeak out, "What?"

The guy zips up and gives me that pity look—you know the one. It says thank God I'm not you, in the nicest way possible. "You're in the men's room. The women's room is down the hall."

This can't be happening. Horrified, I lunge for my books, but he steps to the counter to pick them up at the same time. We collide and his firm body smacks into mine. I stutter something incoherent, finally getting a good look at his face. Holy hotness! I never look at other guys, but once in a while someone that is supermodel perfect catches my attention. When people like that cross your path, it's impossible to look away. His beauty is blinding, and even through tears I notice his sexy smirk, mildly amused blue eyes, and perfectly smooth skin.

Add in his hard body and holy crap. I smacked into the hottest man I've ever seen, stared at his package, and made an ass out of myself. I'm still upset, but so mortified at the same time, that I no longer think and adrenaline takes over. Heart pounding, I push off his firm chest and right myself. My mouth dangles open as I try to form words, but my balance sucks and my hip bumps the books. They topple off the counter and clatter to the floor, while the rest of my stuff slides into the sink for a swim. I can't be this catastrophe. I can't face this hot guy with raccoon eyes, unable to do anything but grunt at him like a baboon.

There aren't many ways to play off a disaster of these proportions. I decide to do the only respectable thing and run like hell. Before he can say anything else, I'm out the door and down the hall. And we're talking full out run, not that little sissy girl run. I mean full out, an axe murderer is going to chop me up, run.

I hear his voice behind me, calling me to come back. Thank God I didn't put my name in my books, yet. I have enough problems without shit like this happening. Horrified, I think about how freaking weird I had to look standing there, mascara running, just staring at his thingy. I stared. What the hell is wrong with me? Who does stuff like that?

I shove through the door at the end of the hall and fly down the stairwell. I'm outside and into the parking lot before I slow down. Rasping for air, I round the side of the building and double over, struggling to breathe. I stand for a second before sliding my back down the wall and pulling my knees to my chest. I bury my face and let the tears fall.

## Chapter 2

"Hey?" The voice is coming from my left. I spot a Chinese Slipper out of the corner of my eye and a long blue skirt. "Are you all right?"

I don't glance up. "Yeah. I'm fine." I've been sitting on the side of the building for a while. I completely blew off my art class. Great first day. Even if I can make it to my dorm room, I can't cry there because the roommate from Hell might walk in.

Slipper Girl sits down next to me and gives a gentle laugh. "Dude, you're a really bad liar."

"I know." We both offer up a nervous laugh. I chance it and peek out at her. I know I look terrible. My face is puffy and smeared with makeup. I'm pretty sure my jeans are covered in snot. It's one of those moments where you wish you had the power of invisibility, but I don't. And she sees me. I haven't made a single friend since I got here, so I feel weird actually talking to someone. I give her a weak half-smile.

She pulls her knees into her chest, and wraps her arms around her ankles. The little black slippers stick out from under her skirt. "So, I'm thinking we need emergency ice cream and maybe—a frying pan."

What? I sit up a little bit and look at her. Slipper Girl has a pretty face and light brown hair that flows like a silky curtain from the top of her head to her waist. It's really long. "What's the frying pan for?"

"To smack the guy who made you cry like that on your first day."

I sniffle and swipe my eyes with the back of my hand. "Oh, I thought we were going to make stir fry."

She smiles at me. "You can cook?" She reaches into her little woven purse and hands me a tissue.

"Not really. I'm pretty good at burning things and making food that's easy to cook but tastes really gross. How about you?"

"Eh," she tilts her hand back and forth. "So-so, but I make some badass cookies. They're orgasmic. Seriously. I'm the cookie queen." She laughs and looks bashful, which makes me smile. "So, since cooking dinner sounds less than tasty, there's this great Chinese place near here. Are you hungry?" The girl tucks a lock of hair behind her ear and motions to a nearby parking lot. "My car is right over there. We could eat and be back before the next class begins. What do you say?"

"I look like a train wreck."

"Yeah, you don't know this about me, but I'm not taking no for an answer. Everyone tells me yes. To everything. I'm spoiled rotten." She grins and flashes all her teeth before standing. Holding out her hand, she says, "Come on. I won't bite and I have an emergency Guys-Suck pack in my car. It has cookies, Midol, concealer, a baseball cap, and a pack of condoms. We can make balloon animals. I make a mean giraffe."

Wiping my eyes with the back of my hand, I say, "You had me at orgasmic cookies."

She laughs and helps me up. "They are. You better be ready, otherwise you'll be blushing, I'll have to pretend it isn't awkward, and we won't be able to look at each other. That's pretty lame, right?"

"Yeah, I have enough people to avoid eye contact with right now, anyway." A small smile spreads across my face, and my cheeks suddenly burn.

"I sense a story, here. What happened? You

have to tell me."

"Nothing," I hedge, but a smile tugs at my lips and a fresh blush burns under my cheeks.

"You can totally tell me! I won't say a word." I follow her to a new white Volvo parked at the back of the lot. She throws her bag in the back seat as I get in on the passenger side. "Oh, dude—my name is Beth. Beth means keeper of secrets." She shoots me a winning smile and starts the car.

"I'm Kerry."

"So, spill. What's your major and all that?" She starts the car and pulls out of the parking lot.

"I'm Kerry Hill, an art major from New York. My boyfriend dumped me this morning via text message, and I was so upset that I mistakenly walked into the men's bathroom right before class. While there, I bumped into a super-hot guy, saw his, uh—package—and stared. After that, I made friends with the brick wall until you came along. It's a pretty pathetic first day of college."

Her jaw drops and she stares at me for way too long. Since we're in moving traffic, it's alarming. The girl is the worst driver I've ever seen. I'm having trouble not screaming. The light is yellow and about to flip to red and she's not slowing down. "You have me beat. Beth

Gallub from Seattle, the youngest of four siblings, with three overprotective brothers that follow me everywhere. Ten bucks says one of them shows up before your class later. No joke."

"Awh, you're the baby."

"Psh. Yeah. It sucks monkeys, man. What about you? Do you have siblings?"

"Yeah, an older brother and a younger sister."

"So, you're the pathologically needy middle child."

"Psych major?"

She laughs. "How'd you know?"

"A hunch. You seem like the kind of person who can't pass a crying chick on the sidewalk." I laugh and the rest of my nerves flutter away. I relax as much as I can pretend to with Beth driving. Seriously. People in Seattle must not think lines are important. The girl is all over the road.

Finally, she pulls into the parking lot for the Chinese restaurant. We get out, head into the buffet and grab a table.

After we eat and talk about our horrible first days—mine takes the loser cake—Beth leans back in the booth and watches me. "So, it's rebound night, right?"

I shift in my seat and scrunch my face.

"Not unless we're talking about a cake rebound."

Beth shakes her head. "The fastest way to get over a broken heart isn't a lifetime in a shrink's chair, it's screwing another guy. That severs the connection, so the next time you meet a guy you're really into you won't compare him to your ex. If you still feel an emotional connection to your ex, you'll compare sex with the new guy to sex with your ex—which will make you an emotional basket case." She pauses for a second, then leans forward, a curious expression on her face. "What do you usually do to get over a guy?"

This feels personal and the urge to make something up comes over me, but I don't do it. Instead, I tell her the lameball truth. "I haven't broken up like this before. We were together for a long time." My eyes drop to the table and my throat tightens, but there are no more tears. I won't cry for him again, but that doesn't ease the pain flowing from the center of my chest.

"Oh, that's rough." Beth glances over my shoulder and waves at someone. I don't turn, because it's just a passing gesture. She didn't wave the person over, but before I know it, there's a guy standing at the table. Beth rolls her eyes. "What did I tell you? This is my brother, Josh. One of them. This is Kerry. Note the boobs. She's a chick. Now, leave me alone."

My face turns bright red when she directs him to look at my chest, but he seems to be used to her antics. At least I hope that's it, because he doesn't look. Josh is a nice looking guy and faintly resembles Beth. He's on the shorter side, built with broad shoulders and gold-streaked brown hair. It's pulled back into a ponytail. "When you didn't show up, Justin asked me to check on you."

Beth groans and fake shoots herself in the head, before falling sideways into the booth, and then disappears under the table. "I have my own life," she whines from the bench.

"Obviously. You're very mature." Josh flashes a smile my way and slips into the booth next to me. I slide over and Beth sits up, a plastic smile on her face.

"I am," she says, smoothing her skirt and raising both her eyebrows excessively high. "Kerry and I were discussing rebound sex. Would you like to enlighten us with your wisdom regarding the best course of action following a break up?" She folds her hands on the tabletop and smiles like a deranged secretary.

Josh laughs once and looks over at me. "Was your relationship serious?"

"Very," Beth answers for me. "What's the best way to move on?"

He looks at me a moment longer than I expect him to. "I don't know you, Kerry, but the only way to get over anyone is to move on. Rebounding is one way, but—"

Beth cuts him off. "But it's not for the faint of heart. Oh my God. You're such a dick. There's no way in hell that I'm letting her hook up with you, assface, so drop it." For a second I think Beth is being too harsh. He wasn't going to hit on me, but then Josh laughs and relaxes.

He bumps his shoulder against mine. "Fine, but I had to try. She's hot." Glancing over at me he says, "Have sex with a stranger to cut the cords and wipe the slate clean. It's the fastest way out of the hellhole you're in right now. And I strongly suggest you pick the guy or some dickwad will play you."

"Like you?" Beth asks, sticking out her tongue at him. Josh smiles.

"Exactly like me, and since I know Beth, you'd have to see me again, which would suck. My advice—pick a guy from a bar on the other side of the city, making the odds of running into him again unlikely." He swipes Beth's glass and downs the rest of her soda.

"So, people really do this? No one think I'm a slut? It seems kind of crazy to walk up to some guy and say, what? I need to get laid. Wanna have sex with me?" This conversation is making me really uncomfortable.

Josh laughs. "Well, don't say it like that. You sound crazy. You need to make him think you've done it before or you'll set off his psycho-bitch alert."

"Guys don't have that, Josh. And does it really matter what she says? No one listens after they hear 'do you want sex?'" Beth tilts her head to the side and makes a face, like she thinks guys are mindless zombie folk.

"You should tell him that you're not looking for a relationship and ask him if he wants to do something. Let him offer." Josh turns to me and studies the side of my face. "You've only been with one guy?"

I nod. "Yeah."

"Was he good? Ouch! Beth, what the hell?" He shifts next to me and clutches his leg under the table.

"You can't ask her that! I met her, like, an hour ago and you're already asking if her ex satisfied her sexually? God, Josh! Go to the store and buy some manners."

Josh cringes. "I didn't say it like that."

The two of them are like a comedy act. I can tell they love each other, but they both have very different, chaffing personalities. "It's okay," I offer, and they stop squabbling and look at me. "I don't have a reference point outside of my ex—he was my first and only."

Beth looks horrified. "You thought you were going to be together forever, didn't you? Oh my God. Josh, don't be a dick, hug her."

I laugh nervously and scoot toward the wall, "Yeah, that's okay. I really don't—well, okay." Before I can get away, Josh throws his arms around me and squeezes hard, mashing my body against his in a bear of a side-hug. I choke, "I'm fine. Really."

"You poor kid!" He releases me and slips out. "Beth, I can head out there with you after seven. If you want to go before then, call Jace."

Beth's jaw tightens and she doesn't look at him. "You're not coming."

Josh smirks and chuckles. "You're funny." He kisses the top of her head and Beth mashes her lips together like she's going to explode. "See you ladies tonight. Oh, and Kerry—dress like you want a good time." He winks at me and rushes out.

**SECRETS & LIES, Vol. 1**
**is available now! Buy it today!**

# COMING SOON

THE ARRANGEMENT, Vol. 21

***** 

To ensure you don't miss H.M. Ward's next book, text AWESOMEBOOKS (one word) to 22828 and you will get an email reminder on release day.

*****

**Want to talk to other fans?**
Go to *Facebook* and join the discussion!

# MORE FERRO FAMILY BOOKS

## NICK FERRO
*~THE WEDDING CONTRACT~*
*****

## BRYAN FERRO
*~THE PROPOSITION~*
*****

## SEAN FERRO
*~THE ARRANGEMENT~*
******

## PETER FERRO GRANZ
*~DAMAGED~*
******

## JONATHAN FERRO
*~STRIPPED~*
******

# MORE ROMANCE BY H.M. WARD

*SCANDALOUS*

*SCANDALOUS 2*

*SECRETS*

*THE SECRET LIFE OF TRYSTAN SCOTT*

*DEMON KISSED*

CHRISTMAS KISSES

*SECOND CHANCES*

And more.

To see a full book list, please visit:
*www.sexyawesomebooks.com/#!/BOOKS*

# CAN'T WAIT FOR H.M. WARD'S NEXT STEAMY BOOK?

★★★★★

Let her know by leaving stars and telling her what you liked about
**THE ARRANGEMENT 20**
in a review!

# COVER REVEAL: